Danny's Big Adventure

written and photographed
by
Mia Coulton

For Rob, a.k.a. Dad

Danny's Big Adventure

Published by:
MaryRuth Books Inc.
P.O. Box 221143
Beachwood, Ohio 44122
216-491-0261

Printed In China

www.maryruthbooks.com

ISBN 0-9746475-0-0

Contents

The Trip

Bang! Bang! Bang!

Something is different
this morning.

Dad is making a lot of noise.

I see some luggage.

It's Dad's luggage.

Dad is going away.

Dad is going on a trip.

"Take me, too!

Take me, too!

Take me to the beach," I bark.

"I am not going

to the beach, Danny.

I do not want

to go ride the waves,"

says Dad.

"I want to ride horses!

I'm going out West!"

"Take me, too!

Please, take me, too,"

I bark again.

Dad sits down beside me.

He pats my head and smiles.

I wag my tail.

I lick his face again and again.

"Don't worry," he tells me.

"You are going to stay

with Abby and her family.

You'll have a good time."

"It will be fun.

Think of it as a **Big Adventure**.

Now, go get your backpack."

I open my backpack.

I put in my bowl.

I put in my food.

Bee is in

my backpack, too.

I am ready

for a **Big Adventure**.

Dad starts to laugh,

"Danny, you are going

to need more food than that!

You're staying at Abby's house

for two weeks."

"You need a bigger bag

of food for two weeks.

You eat a lot of food."

Now I am ready to go.

I know I will miss Dad.

I know I will miss my bed.

I also know I will have fun

with Abby.

I guess it's okay.

I jump in the car.

Off we go!

Off we go to Abby's house.

Dad gives me

a big hug.

He tells me

he will take

a lot of pictures

on his trip out West.

He tells me he will be

home in two weeks.

Off he goes.

Off Dad goes

on his trip out West.

Abby and I

are so happy together.

We run up the stairs,

two at a time.

We jump on the bed.

This is so much fun.

"No jumping on the bed,"
we hear someone call
from downstairs.
"Quiet down and go to sleep."

Abby is fast asleep.

I can hear her snore.

I am thinking about Dad.

I miss Dad, but I know

he will be home soon.

I close my eyes.

I start to count sheep.

One,

two,

three...

This is not working.

I can still hear Abby snore.

I start to count snores.

One,

two,

three...z z z z z.

The Park

The sun is shining

through the window.

I know it is time to get up.

It feels different here.

But I am glad I am here.

Abby and I go downstairs.

No one is awake yet.

So, we go outside to play.

Abby's yard is not as big

as my yard.

It is hard to chase after her.

The gate is open.

We look at each other.

We can smell the park

close by.

Off we go.

Off we go to the park.

It is not hard to find our way

to the park.

We go to the

park all the time with Dad.

First, we go north

until we get to the

big tree trunk.

Next, we go west for

one mile.

We're here!

We're here!

Now we can play chase.

Now I can run fast.

Catch me if you can, Abby!

Abby can see a stick in the pond.

She jumps into the water.

She loves to swim.

She puts the stick in her mouth
and brings it to me.

It is beginning
to get dark
outside and
we have to
go home.

It is easy
to find our way home.
We know to go
the opposite way we came.
We go east for one mile.
At the big tree trunk,
we turn south.

We get to Abby's house

and it is late.

Her mom is waiting for us.

She does not look happy.

My heart starts to thump

and my legs start to shake.

Abby has her tail between her

legs and has a sad face.

Yup, she's mad at us.

She tells us we are "bad dogs"

for leaving without her.

We promise

we won't run away again.

It doesn't feel good

when she is mad at us.

Home, Sweet Home

It's Dad!

It's Dad!

Dad is home

from his trip out West.

He has something for me.

Boots.

Cowboy boots from out West.

He has something for Abby, too.

A hat.

A cowboy hat from out West.

I want to go home right now.

I can't wait to sleep

in my own bed.

I can't wait to play

in my own yard.

I hurry and get my backpack.

Good-bye Abby's house.

My bed looks

just like I left it.

I start to circle around

and around.

Plop.

I'm right in the center

of my bed.

I put my head down

to have a nap with Bee.

Bee!

Where's Bee?

I need Bee!

I need to find Bee right now.

I need to go back to Abby's.

I race down the stairs

and out the door.

I see Abby.

What is in her mouth?

It's yellow and black

and has

two big eyes.

It's Bee!

Thank you, Abby.

Now I can go to sleep.

I circle around

and around.

Plop.

I'm right in the center

of my bed.

I put my head down

to have a nap with Bee.

Ahhh...

I can hear

Dad downstairs.

He is listening

to some music.

It sounds like cowboy music.

Dad is singing,

"I'm an old cowhand,

from the Rio Grande..."

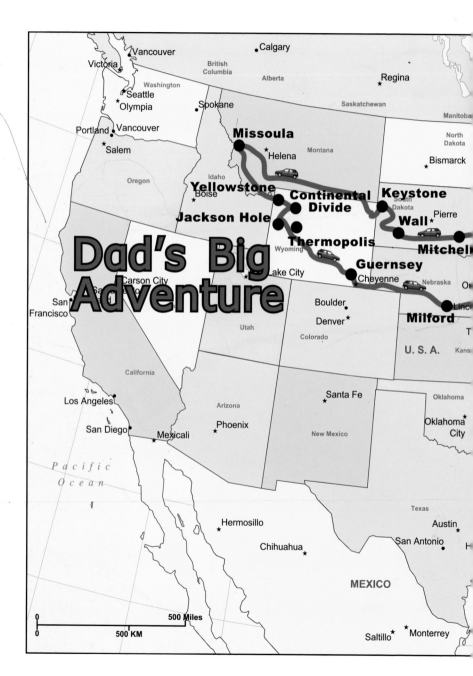

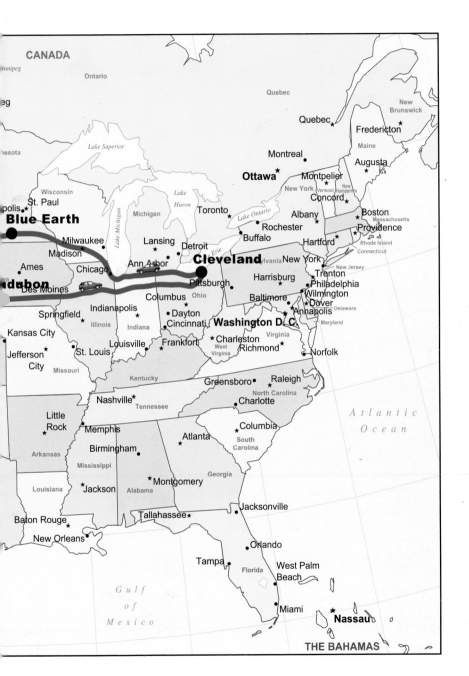

CANADA

Winnipeg

eg

Ontario

Quebec

nnesota

Lake Superior

New Brunswick

Quebec

Fredericton

Montreal

Maine

Augusta

Ottawa

Montpelier

Wisconsin

St. Paul

polis

Blue Earth

Lake Huron

Michigan

Toronto

Lake Ontario

New York Vermont New Hampshire

Concord

Albany

Rochester

Boston

Massachusetts

Providence

Milwaukee

Lansing

Detroit

Buffalo

Hartford

Rhode Island

Madison

Lake Michigan

Ann Arbor

Erie

Cleveland

lvania

New York

Connecticut

Ames

Chicago

Pittsburgh

Harrisburg

Trenton

New Jersey

udubon

Des Moines

Columbus

Ohio

Baltimore

Philadelphia

Wilmington

Dover

Springfield

Indianapolis

Dayton

Cincinnati

Washington D.C.

Annapolis

Delaware

Illinois

Indiana

Maryland

Kansas City

Louisville

Frankfort

Charleston

Virginia

Jefferson City

St. Louis

Missouri

Kentucky

West Virginia

Richmond

Norfolk

Nashville

Tennessee

Greensboro

Raleigh

North Carolina

Little Rock

Memphis

Charlotte

Columbia

Arkansas

Birmingham

Atlanta

South Carolina

Mississippi

Jackson

Montgomery

Georgia

Alabama

Louisiana

A t l a n t i c

O c e a n

Baton Rouge

Tallahassee

Jacksonville

New Orleans

Orlando

Tampa

Florida

West Palm Beach

G u l f

o f

M e x i c o

Miami

Nassau

THE BAHAMAS

"Danny, come quick,"

Dad calls.

"Come and look at my

photo album from out West."

Dad laughs and says,

"Guess who's big feet these are?"

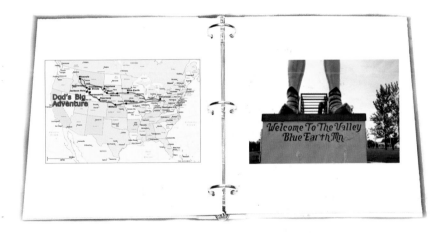

Blue Earth, Minnesota

It's the Jolly Green Giant.

I think he is bigger than Danny!

The statue is 55 feet tall.

Mitchell, South Dakota

Three thousand bushels of corn cover the Mitchell Corn Palace. I would never let Danny near this building when he is hungry.

Wall, South Dakota

No trip out West is complete without a stop at the Wall Drug Store. Did you know Wall Drug is famous because it gives out free ice water and free bumper stickers?

Keystone, South Dakota

Mount Rushmore is located in the Black Hills of South Dakota. The faces of four presidents (George Washington, Thomas Jefferson, Abraham Lincoln, Theodore Roosevelt) are carved in stone. Washington's nose is bigger than a car!

Missoula, Montana

Smokejumpers are firefighters who parachute out of planes and into forest fires. Often they are the first to reach the fires. Their tools, food and water are dropped by parachute after they land.

Yellowstone, Wyoming

Here is a real moose. Don't get too close, Danny. In Yellowstone Park, a lot of moose are on the loose.

Continental Divide

Which way do I go, Danny?

All rivers to the west of the

Continental Divide flow to the

Pacific Ocean. All the rivers to

the east flow to the Atlantic

Ocean. Is that cool or what?

Jackson Hole, Wyoming

I am pointing to the Grand Teton.

It's the highest mountain here.

Now, that would be a long hike

for Danny and me.

Thermopolis, Wyoming

Wow! A natural hot spring.

The water comes up from the

ground and is hot all year round.

Get your swimsuit.

Guernsey, Wyoming

I'm in a rut. That's right, a rut.

So many wagons traveled the

Oregon Trail that their wheels cut

ruts into solid rock. The ruts are

still here today, more than

100 years later.

Milford, Nebraska

Oh my stars!

The world's largest covered

wagon. This is one site I could

have skipped. Now it is a

motorcycle shop.

Audubon, Iowa

This is Albert, the world's largest

bull. His frame was built with

steel taken from old, abandoned

Iowa windmills.

Now that's recycling.

"So Danny, what do you think

of my Big Adventure?"

"Danny...?"

"Danny...?"